For my darling Nathaniel, so, so much.

And for my nephews Leo and Orion,
two of the hungriest little lions I know.

ATHENEUM BOOKS FOR YOUNG READERS

An imprint of Simon & Schuster Children's Publishing Division

1230 Avenue of the Americas, New York, New York 10020

ATHENEUM BOOKS FOR YOUNG READERS is a registered trademark of Simon & Schuster, Inc.

Atheneum logo is a trademark of Simon & Schuster, Inc.

For information about special discounts for bulk purchases, please contact Simon & Schuster Special Sales
at 1-866-506-1949 or business@simonandschuster.com.

The Simon & Schuster Speakers Bureau can bring authors to your live event. For more information or to
book an event, contact the Simon & Schuster Speakers Bureau at 1-866-248-3049 or visit our website at
www.simonspeakers.com.

Book design by Sonia Chaghatzbanian

The text for this book is set in Baskerville.

The illustrations for this book are rendered in brush marker, gouache, graphite, colored pencil, and charcoal.

Manufactured in China

1215 SCP

First Edition

10 9 8 7 6 5 4 3 2 1

Library of Congress Cataloging-in-Publication Data

Cummins, Lucy Ruth, author, illustrator.

A hungry lion, or a dwindling assortment of animals / Lucy Ruth Cummins. — First edition.

pages cm

Summary: Members of a large group of animals, including a penguin, two rabbits, and a koala, disappear
at an alarming rate but the hungry lion remains.

ISBN 978-1-4814-4889-5 (hardcover) — ISBN 978-1-4814-4890-1 (ebook)

[1. Animals—Fiction. 2. Predatory animals—Fiction. 3. Surprise—Fiction.] I. Title.

PZ7.1.C86Hun 2016

[E]—dc23

2015000523

A HUNGRY LION

or A DWINDLING
ASSORTMENT *of* ANIMALS

written and illustrated by
Lucy Ruth Cummins

Atheneum   Atheneum Books for Young Readers   New York   London   Toronto   Sydney   New Delhi

Once upon a time there was a hungry lion,
a penguin, a turtle, a little calico kitten,
a brown mouse, a bunny with floppy ears
and a bunny with un-floppy ears,
a frog, a bat, a pig, a slightly bigger pig,
a woolly sheep, a koala, and also a hen.

Hold on.

Once upon a time there was a hungry lion,
a penguin, a turtle, a brown mouse,
those two rabbits—
one with ears that flopped,
one with ears that did not—
a frog, a bat, a regular-size pig, a koala, and a hen.

Wait a second.

It seems there was *just* a hungry lion,
a turtle, only the floppy-eared rabbit,
a frog, a bat, and a pig.
And apparently?

No one else.

Umm . . .

I guess Once
upon a time there was just a
HUNGRY LION

and a dwindling assortment
of other animals.

Well. Okay. . . . It seems now we have only:

A HUNGRY LION.

And that turtle.

Hello, there. . . . *Excuse me*—
where did everyone go . . . ?

Ummm . . .

HEY!

Why's it so dark in here??

shhhh...

Hooray!

Once upon a time there was an
enormous, lovely four-tiered cake
with buttercream frosting,
a partying penguin, a twisting turtle,
a calico kitten—who happens
to be shimmying—a brown mouse
(a bit of a wallflower),
two bunnies line dancing, a sheep chatting
with a frog, a bat doing his bat thing, a pair
of pigs squealing with piggish delight,
a contented koala, a happy hen . . .

and . . .

. . . a less hungry lion.

Well, look who's arrived
fashionably late.
A really ravenous T. rex!

Once upon a time there was just a hungry little turtle and a very large cake.